MASTER OF THE BEASTS

TECTON
THE ARMOURED
GIANT

With special thanks to Ellen Renner

To Louis, a big fan

www.beastquest.co.uk

ORCHARD BOOKS
338 Euston Road, London NW1 3BH
Orchard Books Australia
Level 17/207 Kent St, Sydney, NSW 2000

A Paperback Original
First published in Great Britain in 2012

Beast Quest is a registered trademark of Beast Quest Limited
Series created by Beast Quest Limited, London

Text © Beast Quest Limited 2012
Cover and inside illustrations by Steve Sims
© Beast Quest Limited 2012

A CIP catalogue record for this book is available from
the British Library.

ISBN 978 1 40831 522 4

3 5 7 9 10 8 6 4

Printed and bound by CPI Group (UK) Ltd, Croydon, CR0 4YY

Orchard Books is a division of Hachette Children's Books,
an Hachette UK company

www.hachette.co.uk

TectoN
THE ARMOURED
GIANT

BY ADAM BLADE

ORCHARD

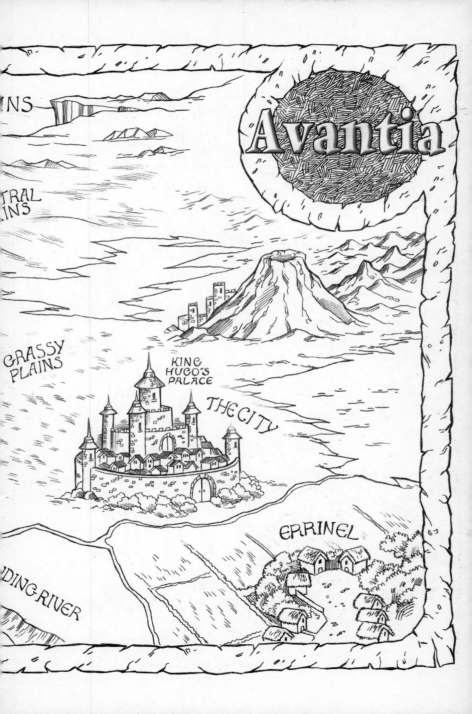

So... You still wish to follow Tom on his Beast Quest.

Turn back now. A great evil lurks beneath Avantia's earth, waiting to arise and conquer the kingdom with violence and rage. Six Beasts with the hearts of Ancient Warriors, at the mercy of the Evil Wizard, Malvel, who I fear has reached the height of his powers.

War awaits us all.

I beg you, again, close this book and turn away. Evil will rise. Darkness will fall.

Your friend,
Wizard Aduro

PROLOGUE

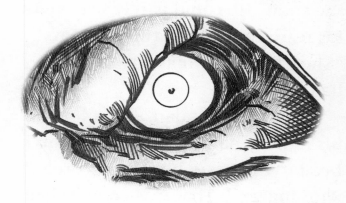

The summer sun hung directly overhead as Albin walked home across the snow with his father, Brendan. The icy plains of Avantia's northland sparkled in the sunlight. Albin tugged his leather sunshield lower over his eyes. *Even the best shooter in the world won't be able to play iceball with snow blindness*, he reminded himself.

"Did you see Melda's save, Dad?" Albin asked, peering up at his father as they crunched side by side through the snow. He could barely believe that his team had beaten the Ice Bears! "She's the best stopper we've ever had."

"Yes," said Brendan. Albin felt his father's hand rest briefly on his head. "And I saw how you scored the winning goal. That was good iceball, son."

Brendan didn't often give praise. Albin glowed with pleasure.

Suddenly, Albin crashed into something as cold as an iceball but hard as iron. He cried out and fell to one knee, holding his stinging nose.

"What is it, son? Did you slip?" Brendan asked as he reached down to help Albin to his feet.

"No," said Albin. He squinted through the slits in his sunshield, trying to see what he had walked into. The air in front of him seemed to shimmer and shift and a faint outline of silvery armour appeared. A white knight was blocking their path, almost invisible against the snow and ice.

"Greetings, noble Sir!" Brendan said hastily. "I apologise for my son. He didn't see you."

Albin stared at the knight in awe. His heart thudded with excitement. *I bet he's on a dangerous mission for the king*, he thought. *I wonder if he needs a boy to help him?*

"I am looking for the Beast called Nanook!" The knight's voice scratched through the silence like a rusty knife. The blank white visor turned towards Brendan.

Albin gasped. Few people knew

about the existence of the Beasts.
The only reason he and his father
did was because a hero called Tom
had once visited the Northlands and
saved them from disaster. Albin and
Brendan owed Tom their lives.

Albin looked at his father and saw
Brendan's mouth tighten.

"Why do you want to find the
Beast?" he asked, his voice quiet
and respectful.

The knight raised an armour-clad
arm as though he meant to strike
Brendan down. "You dare to question
me? Answer! Where is Nanook?"

Brendan bowed his head. "I'll show
you the lair of the great Beast. But
I warn you, she will be hibernating.
Neither she nor those who live here
will thank you if you disturb her.
The last time she was woken from

hibernation, she almost sank the entire northern plain into the waters of the great lake!"

The knight threw back his head and laughter carried across the snowfield. "I promise that Nanook will not move from her lair!" he said.

But there, on the horizon was... "Dad," Albin cried. "Look!" A creature with the face and hairy, hunched shoulders of a hyena stalked across the snow towards them. It was the size of a horse, and sharp yellow tusks curled up from the corners of its grinning mouth. The wild animal was almost upon them...

"Use your iceball stick, Albin!" his father cried, raising his stout wooden walking staff to fend off the animal.

Albin clenched his stick in both hands. His eyes flicked to the stranger.

Surely the knight would help them.

The White Knight did not draw a weapon. Instead, he strolled over to the giant hyena. His grating voice echoed back to them. "Don't be afraid of my Varkule. It won't harm you unless I command it to." Another slow laugh chilled Albin's blood, and the boy saw his father stiffen and step backwards.

The creature paused a few steps away. The smell of rotting flesh hung in the air around it. Albin felt his stomach tighten as he saw a pair of long white ears disappear between the Varkule's leathery lips. The hideous thing had just eaten a snow rabbit.

Brendan began to back them away from the knight and his pet Varkule. "I...I find I cannot remember where

Nanook's lair is," Albin's father stuttered. "I am sorry, but my son and I must be on our way now. There are chores to be done…"

Brendan's voice trailed away. Albin watched as the White Knight lifted his visor. His face was skeletal. Two sunken eyes burned in deep sockets. The knight grinned at them, his rotting, blackened teeth dark as lumps of charcoal against his shining white armour.

Albin opened his mouth to scream, but his voice was frozen in terror. The knight's body was swelling, growing impossibly large. The Varkule backed away, cowering, as the knight grew to five times the size of a man. The sound of screeching metal filled the air as the shining white armour dulled to the colour of lead.

The knight's body grew round and high-backed. He dropped onto four stumpy legs with a thud that shook the ground beneath Albin's feet. His helmeted head stretched into a long black snout and his body grew a thick hide of armoured plates studded with deadly spikes.

No weapon could possibly dent that armour! Albin thought.

Brendan must have realised this too. He whirled Albin around and

gave him a shove. "Run, Albin!'
he shouted. 'Run for your life!"

Fear chased Albin across the snow
and ice. He could hear his father
panting at his side. But he could also
make out another noise: a rumbling,
growing louder and louder. *It's the
Beast,* Albin thought. *It's after us!*

Unable to stop himself, Albin
glanced over his shoulder.

The Beast was chasing them. But
it wasn't running! It had curled itself
up like a giant, spiked hedgehog and
was rolling after them at great speed
– too fast to escape. Albin stared as
the enormous whirling ball careered
towards him. He knew he had no
chance at all...

CHAPTER ONE

INTO THE COLD

Tom and Elenna stood in a fringe of pine trees on the brow of a hill. Below them stretched a rolling plain of snow and ice. The marble globe map given to Tom had led them to the edge of Avantia's frozen northlands. This was where they would meet the next Knight of Forton…and the next Beast: *Tecton!*

Tom's stallion, Storm, snorted and

stamped his feet but stood still as Tom pulled two cloaks from the saddlebag. They had bartered the last of their precious apples for these in the last town. The northerners had plenty of furs but they seldom saw fresh fruit.

Tom tossed a cloak to Elenna, who fastened it around her neck and pulled the hood up to cover her head. "Warmer already," she said, reaching down to pat her wolf, Silver. "See, I have fur now too."

Tom wrapped himself in his cloak. Taking Storm's reins, he led them all downhill. The last of the trees and grass disappeared. As soon as he stepped onto the snow, Tom felt cold bite at the uncovered skin of his face and hands. His breath frosted to ice crystals.

Before him stretched a world of white beneath a bright blue sky, shimmering in the sunlight. Tom found himself squinting and he tugged his hood forwards to shade his eyes. His boots broke through a crust of soft snow to the hard packed layers below. Elenna marched at his side, the crunch of her footsteps echoing his own.

Tom had tied a horse blanket on the stallion's back. He could only hope it would keep his friend warm enough.

"Look!" Elenna said. Through the dazzling light Tom could just make out a tall figure striding towards the horizon. At this distance, the stranger was a mere shadow against the glaring white, but something about the way he moved seemed familiar to Tom. He'd seen that stride before. *Of course!* he thought. *It's another knight.*

But before Tom could give chase, the figure vanished out of sight.

Six knights had been brought back to hideous life by Malvel's evil spell. The knights had been liberated from the Gallery of Tombs, but they no longer resembled their former selves. Each possessed the power to transform into the Beast they had once defeated. *Only a truly twisted mind could have thought of that*, Tom thought.

The knight he'd just seen would be no different. Out there somewhere was an ancient warrior waiting to transform into a powerful Beast – a Beast that Tom must face and defeat before it could hunt down and destroy Nanook.

The cold grew more intense as they pushed deeper into the heart of the snow plain. Tom shivered and walked faster. He glanced at Elenna and she nodded cheerfully, but he saw that her lips were turning blue with cold.

Tom glanced to his left and saw a line of shadows in the snow: a trail of footsteps. "Elenna, over there!" Tom pointed.

"It must be the person we saw," Elenna said, standing beside Tom as he examined the marks.

"Yes, but look," said Tom. "The footsteps *begin* here, in the middle of the snow field." He pointed to the first set of footsteps. The snow behind them was smooth and unbroken.

"But..." Elenna shook her head. "That means whoever made them must have dropped out of the sky!"

"I don't know what it means," said Tom. He followed the line of footprints with his eye until they disappeared into the distance. "But our path takes us the same way. We need to be prepared." Beneath his cloak, he rested his hand on the hilt of his sword.

They walked on, following the line of footprints. The gentle downward swell of the snowy banks flattened out. Tom realised they had reached the edge of an enormous frozen lake. From now on, they would be travelling over Avantia's famous ice plains.

It was even colder on the ice. The places where the wind had scoured the surface clear of snow were treacherous underfoot. Tom found his feet threatening to slide out from under him more than once. Storm picked his way carefully. The stallion seemed to know instinctively where it was safe to walk. Tom glanced at Elenna and saw that she was beginning to shiver.

"We must find shelter," he said.

Elenna nodded and Tom picked up the pace. Walking faster would help them keep warm. The snow glare was even worse now, and his eyes were beginning to ache. He peered ahead, trying to catch another glimpse of the mysterious figure. Instead, he spotted a building on the horizon – the low mound of a house built on a section of land protruding into the frozen lake. It was half covered in snow but a curl of smoke rose from its chimney.

"There's our shelter," Tom said, pointing to the building.

"Good," Elenna said. "Perhaps they will have seen the White Knight."

They hurried across the ice to the lonely dwelling – a small single storey building made of thick stone. Icicles dangled like frozen fingers from the roof. As Tom approached, he saw that the door was made from heavy steel.

"This place is like a fortress!" he said. "It only has one window and it's as narrow as an arrow slit."

"Built to keep intruders out and warmth inside," Elenna replied. "But surely they'll give us shelter."

"Storm, wait here," Tom ordered his stallion.

"And you, Silver," Elenna told her wolf.

The two animals began to trot in circles in order to stay warm. Tom smiled: clever creatures! He raised his hand to knock on the door.

"Wait!" Elenna grabbed his arm. "Listen! Someone in there is hurt!"

Tom heard it too: a low groaning. He glanced at Elenna.

"They need help," she said. But he noticed she had unslung her bow and was pulling an arrow from her quiver.

"Let's hope that's all it is," Tom replied. It crossed his mind that the mysterious stranger they had seen in the distance might have prepared a clever trap. *Well,* he thought, *there's only one way to find out.* Tom drew his sword and pushed open the door of the house.

CHAPTER TWO

OLD FRIENDS AND A NEW ENEMY

Tom stepped into warmth and blinding darkness. As his eyes adjusted, he saw a small room with a metal stove against one wall. A table and chairs stood in the centre, and in one corner a man lay on a low bed. A small boy bent over him.

The boy jerked around, his eyes wide with fear.

Tom recognised him at once: it was Albin, a friend he met on one of his first Quests. And the man on the bed was Brendan, Albin's father.

Tom slid his sword into its scabbard. Elenna rushed to Brendan's side, her arrow already back in its quiver.

"He's badly wounded," she said.

"Tom! Elenna!" Albin's face crumpled with relief. He gazed at Tom, his eyes bright with hope. "You've come to defeat the bad Beast. I knew you would. But please, help my father!"

"We'll try our best," Tom said, striding to the bedside. Brendan's face was pale, his clothes bloody and torn, his body covered with deep cuts. He moaned softly. His eyes flickered open and rested on Tom's face without recognition. Then Brendan's eyes shut and his breath grew harsh and laboured. Tom frowned, glancing at Albin's hopeful face. *Are we too late to save his father?*

Tom pulled Epos's talon from his shield and held it over Brendan – the talon had the power to heal cuts and bruises. Tom hoped its magic would be enough to save him. He concentrated on directing its healing power into the wounded man.

As soon as he touched the talon to Brendan's skin, Tom saw the cuts begin to close and heal to shiny scars. The man's face lost its waxy pallor. After a few moments, his eyes opened. This time, when he saw Tom bending over him, Brendan smiled with pleasure.

"Tom!" The man struggled to sit up. "It's good to see you. Let me

make you a hot drink. You look half-
frozen."

"Stay quiet, Father," said Albin. His
face was shiny with tears of joy. Tom
glanced from him to Elenna, who was
smiling in delight.

"I'll heat the kettle." Albin gripped his father's hand for a moment, and then darted to the kitchen.

Brendan was looking healthier by the second, but he was frowning with worry. "Tom, you must be careful. There's an evil knight in armour as white as snow stalking the ice plain. He keeps a giant creature as a pet. Like a hyena, but—"

"A Varkule!" Tom said, his heart sinking.

"That was what he called it," Brendan said with a nod. "But the Varkule, bad as it is, is not the worst. The White Knight himself transforms into a Beast. Huge and covered in deadly spikes. It wears armour so thick no sword can cut it. The wounds I received from the spikes would have killed me, if you hadn't cured me. You must take care, Tom. Your sword will be useless against the Beast."

"I'll think of something," Tom said, refusing to be disheartened. "I will defeat the Beast. I must!"

"You should find the other Knight," said Albin, looking up from the pot he was stirring. "He might be able to help you."

"What other knight?" Elenna asked, turning to Brendan.

Brendan leaned forward, his eyes gleaming with excitement. "We saw a second knight in the distance as we arrived home. But this one wore a suit of golden armour. It glinted in the sun."

Tom felt a chill finger slide up his spine. Had the last two Knights of Forton teamed up?

"Two?" Elenna looked horrified. "Two Knights of Forton and two Beasts to fight?"

"Even you can't do that, Tom," Brendan said.

"Tom can do anything!" Albin said as he carried a tray of steaming cups over. He handed them round and Tom took his gratefully, sipping the nettle tea and feeling warmth seep into his body.

"Thanks, Albin," Tom said, smiling at Albin and hiding his own fears.

"Listen, Tom..." Elenna began in a low voice. Then she paused and her eyes grew wide with alarm. "The animals!" she cried and sprang to her feet.

Tom heard it too. Silver was howling and Storm neighed in fear. Tom's heart lurched. He jumped up, drawing his sword. The wolf gave a sudden shrill yelp. Then silence fell.

As Tom raced for the door with Elenna at his side, an ear-splitting noise of scratching and grinding erupted. It sounded like the claws and teeth of a large animal raking at the house's steel door. The creature was grunting and panting. The metal door groaned and creaked. Albin cried out in fear.

BANG!

The door burst open and an icy blast of wind roared through the tiny house. With it came the Varkule. It swiped at the door, ripping it from the hinges. The creature filled the room with the stink of dead flesh.

Its eyes glowed red as it spotted Tom. It snarled, revealing a row of

vicious teeth. The snarl turned into
the choking laugh of a hyena as the
Varkule leapt into the room.

CHAPTER THREE

A NEW ENEMY

"Stay back!" Tom shouted at Albin and Brendan. As they cowered on Brendan's bed, he swung his sword at the Varkule's neck. The creature shouldered the sword aside and lunged for him. Tom struck its head with a ringing blow, using the flat of his sword. He only just had time to dodge the sharp teeth that snapped in his face.

Tom beat off the Varkule's furious attacks, but there wasn't room in the tiny house to fight properly. He saw Elenna edge forwards, bowstring drawn back. The point of her arrow followed the Varkule's head as it lunged for Tom, but she couldn't get a clear shot.

The Varkule growled. Yellow drool hung in strands from its teeth. It grunted and snapped at Tom. He stabbed down with his sword, but the Varkule swerved its head away. Elenna darted forwards. She had put her bow down and held a cooking pot in her hands. She swiped at the Varkule, hitting it a ringing blow to the head.

The monster bellowed and staggered back. Tom leapt forward and slashed at the creature's flank.

The Varkule roared in pain, its eyes flaring red. It reared up and whipped its head towards Tom. The force of the blow knocked Tom flying. He hit the wall and pain slammed into his body as he crashed through the bricks and out onto the icy plain.

Tom slid to a stop. His back felt like it was on fire where it had struck the wall, and his head was swimming. He staggered to his feet, glad to find his sword still grasped in his hand. But there was no time to get his breath: his friends were trapped in the house with a Varkule! Its roars thundered across the ice. Tom raced over, fearing the worst.

His heart lurched with relief as he saw first Albin and then Brendan scramble through the hole his body had made in the wall. They turned to

help Elenna slide out. The Varkule's
sharp yellow teeth snapped and
scratched after her. It squeezed its
head through the hole, trying to force
a way through, twisting and snapping
its jaws in frustration. Then it snarled
and pulled its head back inside.

The doorway had collapsed. The creature could not get out that way. But Tom knew that the Varkule would not stay trapped for long. Inside the house, the monster's bellows grew louder. Tom heard the sound of crashing, and the damaged wall shook and buckled. The Varkule would crash through after them any minute. There was only one way to stop it.

Tom pulled the purple jewel he had won from the Beast, Sting, out of his belt. Its magic allowed him to cut through stone. Harnessing its power, he dug his sword into the base of the house. He panted with effort as he circled the dwelling, carving deep into the foundations.

Tom stepped back as the walls of the house shuddered and groaned. The Varkule's howl of fury rang out over

the ice plain. With a grinding rumble,
the walls of the building fell inwards.
The heavy stone roof collapsed, sending
up choking clouds of dust and burying
the creature in a pile of rubble.

Elenna ran to Tom's side and stared
at the remains of Brendan's house.

A few small stones shifted as the heap settled. A dust cloud drifted away on the wind. "Is it dead?" she asked.

"I don't know." Tom slid his sword back into its sheath. "But it won't be bothering us for a while." He glanced at Brendan and Albin, making sure father and son were safe. They huddled together, gazing in shock at the remains of their home.

Before he could move to comfort them, Elenna gripped his arm. "The animals!" she said. "Silver?" she called, twisting away to look for her wolf.

Tom darted for the front of the house. "Storm?" he shouted. "Where are you?"

He spotted a dark shape in the snow and ran to where Storm lay stretched on the ground, Silver was crumpled beside him. For a moment, Tom's heart skipped a beat, but then he saw that the horse was still breathing.

"They've been knocked out," Elenna said, as she checked her wolf for injuries. "But Silver doesn't seem badly hurt. How's Storm?"

Tom knelt and stroked the stallion's neck. Storm's eyes flickered and he raised his head and whinnied softly. Tom held the bridle and steadied the horse as he staggered to his feet. "Storm's all right," Tom said. "Just needs to walk around and get warm again." He adjusted the blanket on the stallion and led him in slow circles until the animal was steady on his legs and snorting with pleasure at being reunited with Tom. "Yes," Tom said, patting the horse's neck fondly. "That was one nasty Varkule."

Albin ran up. "Is Storm uninjured?"

he asked, gazing at Storm with admiration.

"He's fine." Tom turned to Brendan, who had joined them. "I'm sorry about your house," he said. "It's a ruin."

"Better the house pulled down than all of us dead." Brendan smiled at Tom. "Three times now you have saved my son and myself. I can never repay my debt to you."

"But where will you and Albin go?" Tom asked. He couldn't leave the father and son alone and unprotected on the ice plain.

"I will take Albin to my brother's house," said Brendan. "It's only a short walk from here. We will be safe there, and when I feel strong again I'll build a new house for us. We should go now. I sense that the weather is about to change." He glanced at the sky, which appeared the same cloudless blue to Tom. "Will you come with us to rest and get warm?"

"Thank you," Tom said. "But we need to go on. Please be careful. The White Knight will not be far away from his Varkule. Get yourselves to safety and stay inside until I have defeated him." He shook Brendan's hand, then Albin's.

Elenna said goodbye to them, then stood beside Tom as they watched father and son trudge off into the icy whiteness. Soon they were out of sight. "Albin is a brave boy," she said. "Will they be all right?"

"I hope so." Tom whistled for Storm, who came trotting up. "But now we must continue with the Quest. We can't stop until we have defeated all the Knights of Forton!"

He held out the globe map. It directed them due north, and soon they were once more following the footprints made by the mysterious stranger. Tom frowned down at them. Had the last Knight of Forton made these – the one in golden armour? Had he teamed up with the White Knight?

The stranger's track continued north. *Towards Nanook's cave,* Tom thought grimly. *If two Knights meant to attack her, she won't be able to defeat them!* Tom felt a chill of foreboding run down his spine.

Tom squinted into glaring whiteness, trying to make out a landmark, but all he could see was a flat desert of ice. He peered up at the sky. Was it his imagination, or was the sun disappearing behind a hazy cloud? Brendan had said the weather would turn – should Tom and Elenna have taken shelter?

Behind him, he heard Storm snort and stamp his feet. Something was bothering the stallion. Mounting unease weighed upon Tom. His hand crept to his sword hilt. He looked at Elenna and saw that she was frowning and glancing over her shoulder.

"There's something coming, isn't there?" Tom asked. "Do you feel it too?" The wind had risen. It stung Tom's face and whipped the hood from his head.

Elenna nodded. "Silver isn't happy," she said. "And neither am I."

Silver stalked at Elenna's side, the ruff of fur at his neck erect, his teeth showing white in a half snarl. Storm continued to shake his head

and snort. Danger lurked ahead.
Tom was sure of it. *Are we walking
into an ambush?* His eyes scanned the
horizon, squinting into the wind. As
he peered through the ice-glare, he
saw something as dangerous as any
Knight. A huge grey cloud appeared
on the horizon, boiling into the sky.
It raced towards them.

"Ice storm!" Tom shouted.

CHAPTER FOUR

REUNION

The storm howled. The first gusts slammed into them, peppering Tom's face with sharp splinters of ice.

"Behind me!" Tom shouted over the roar of the wind. He tore his shield off his back and held it in front of him, concentrating on harnessing the protective power of Nanook's bell, which could protect Tom from extreme cold. Elenna, Storm and

Silver sheltered behind him just as the full power of the gale hit.

Tom staggered as the wind struck the shield like a giant fist – but the power of the bell held. The shield forced the storm to rage harmlessly over their heads and to either side.

"Let's get out of here!" Elenna shouted.

Tom nodded. "We must find shelter," he shouted back. Holding the shield steady, he began to move forward, pushing into the storm.

Tom locked his arms against the force of the storm and pushed with his legs. After only a few dozen steps, his muscles were burning with the effort. How long would he be able to hold off an ice storm single-handed?

Tom peered over the top of the shield. His mouth opened in surprise and he almost dropped it. There, standing in the full force of the storm, was the tiny figure of a man. His armour glowed like a dot of gold in the sunlight.

"That must be the Golden Knight," Tom gasped, squinting to try to see better.

"You can't fight him now!" Elenna cried. "Not in the middle of a raging blizzard."

But Tom didn't think the knight was holding a weapon. He seemed to beckon to Tom with a golden gauntlet, as though inviting him to follow.

"Don't, Tom!" Elenna said. "It could be a trap."

The knight turned and trudged into the storm a few steps, then turned and waited.

"Maybe," said Tom. "But we can't stay here."

"Then let's be on our guard," said Elenna.

Tom began to walk towards the armoured figure, who turned and headed off into the storm, striding effortlessly. Tom marvelled at the power of his armour, which seemed able to shrug off an ice storm as though it were a shower of rain.

The knight led them away to the right, then down an icy slope. Tom's feet slipped as he followed. His arms felt leaden and his legs were beginning to shake. Would he even have the strength for a duel, once they were out of the storm?

Why is he helping us? Tom asked himself.

Tom glanced over his shield and

saw the knight come to a stop beside
a small circular building half-buried
in a snowdrift. The house seemed
to be built from blocks of solid ice.
A round, tunnel-like entrance faced
them and as Tom watched, the knight

disappeared through the opening.

Elenna grabbed his arm. "You can't fight properly in there!" she said. "Even Brendan's cottage was too small. The Varkule nearly had us. A Knight of Forton is a far greater foe than a Varkule!"

"We can't stay out in this storm either," said Tom.

The opening to the igloo was just large enough to shelter Storm and Silver from the worst of the icy blasts. Tom handed his shield to Elenna, shrugged off his cloak and pulled out his sword. He crouched before the wooden door. He imagined the knight lying in wait on the other side, sword drawn, ready to attack.

Tom took a deep breath and kicked the door. It sprang open with a crash. Tom leapt into the room. He crouched low, his sword ready, waiting for an attack.

Startled, Tom stared around the room. The Golden Knight sat in a chair in the corner. Tom lowered his sword, more confused than ever. There was something familiar about the man sitting there, watching him.

The stranger reached up and pulled off his golden helmet. He placed the helmet on the table beside him and looked at Tom. Then he smiled.

"And what sort of welcome is that, son?" the man asked.

Tom gasped. It wasn't Malvel's sixth Golden Knight after all. It was his father, Taladon!

CHAPTER FIVE

ICE AND FIRE

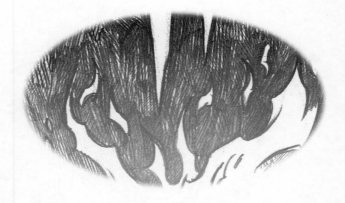

"Father!" Tom's heart leapt with joy. He sheathed his sword and ran to greet Taladon, who rose from his chair with a smile.

Taladon put his arms around Tom and hugged him close. "Welcome, son. It's good to see you. And to see that you take no chances!" His grin widened.

"Well, we didn't know it was you!"

Elenna strode into the room, sliding
an arrow back into her quiver. Her
face lit up with happiness at the sight
of Tom's father. "How did you get
here?"

The last Tom and Elenna had
heard, Taladon was travelling other
kingdoms with Tom's mother, Freya.

Now, he closed the door, shutting out the worst of the wind, and gestured for them to sit on a bench beside the table. He sat back down on the chair and smiled at them. "Aduro summoned me."

"So that's why your footprints looked as though you fell out of the sky!" Elenna cried. "You did!"

"After a fashion. I was in Gwildor, but Aduro told me that your Quest had reached a critical point, Tom. Malvel is planning to re-enter Avantia. I've come to help..." Taladon paused. "If you need me," he added.

Tom grinned at his father. "You're the Master of the Beasts. Of course I want you to fight by my side. The White Knight is nearby. He has a Varkule as a companion, if it still lives. I think he's on the hunt for Nanook."

A bell rang out, its silvery note clear and bright. Tom jumped to his feet and grabbed his shield, which Elenna had placed against a wall. "It's Nanook's bell!" he cried. "She's sending a distress signal! Tecton must be attacking!"

"Then there's no time to lose!" Taladon led the way out of the entrance. The ice storm had rolled on while they were inside and Tom saw the last of it scouring the ice plain in the far distance. He climbed onto Storm and reached down a hand to Elenna, who leapt up behind him.

Tom guided Storm northwards, urging the stallion as fast as he dared over the slippery ice. Silver ran behind, and Taladon, using the power of the Golden Armour, easily kept pace beside them. They travelled quickly, but would they make it in time? Tom felt a surge of relief as he finally spotted Nanook's cave in the distance.

It should have been a beautiful sight, beneath the bright blue sky. But the air above the cave shimmered as though in a heat wave, and Tom gasped. Both ends of the cave were on fire, the flames leaping with a blue-white intensity.

"Nanook is trapped inside!" Tom shouted. *The White Knight has done this!* The thought made him grit his teeth in anger. He urged Storm to go faster.

The stallion cantered up to the nearest entrance, whinnying with fear. Tom rolled swiftly from the saddle. Elenna followed, sprinting with him to the cave entrance. Tom felt a flush of pride as Elenna joined him near the blaze. Her parents had died in a fire when she was a small child and Tom knew it was a struggle for her to come this close to fire.

"What is this wood?' Elenna cried, pointing to the branches piled at the base of the entrance. 'It's totally black, and it doesn't seem to burn up or fall into embers!" The flames roared higher and Elenna flinched backwards. Tom also retreated a step. The edge of his fur-lined cloak was singed and smoking.

"Frishwood." Taladon's voice rang out behind them. Tom turned to see his father's golden armour shimmering in the flickering light of the flames. "Magical and very rare. It's found only in the forests of Rion. Left alone, that Frishwood fire

would burn forever."

Tom stared in amazement. He
thought he'd seen all the wonders
there were, but this was new to him.
And deadly to Nanook! He turned
back to the fire in time to see a large

chunk of ice crumble from the roof of the cave and fall into the fire, which erupted with a gust of hissing steam.

"The roof!" Tom said, pointing. "If the smoke doesn't smother Nanook, the whole cave will collapse."

He reached for his sword, intending to scatter the burning logs.

Whack! Something hit him in the face. Tom cried out and flew backwards across the ice, stunned. He staggered to his feet, his mouth bruised and bleeding. His shield had been torn from his hand, but he didn't have time to search for it now. Instead his eyes searched for any sign of his attacker.

But other than his father and Elenna, who were drawing their weapons, he couldn't see anyone. Tom pulled his sword from its scabbard, looking around. Someone had just attacked him – someone he couldn't see. A single thought taunted him.

How can we fight an invisible foe?

CHAPTER SIX

UNSEEN ENEMY

Taladon stood back to back with Elenna, who had an arrow nocked. Their heads turned as they looked for any sign of the enemy.

"It's the White Knight!" Taladon shouted. "His armour will make him difficult to see against the snow. You must—"

Ooof! Crack! Ooof! With a metallic clash, Taladon's head jerked back as

something struck him a fearsome
blow. He was hit twice more, the
last time with such force that he was
lifted off his feet. Taladon crashed
onto the ice.

Tom ran forwards, squinting against the glare. He thought he saw a shadowy outline of a knight lunge towards Elenna. Before Tom could reach her, the nearly invisible figure swiped at her. Elenna cried out as she tumbled over the ice.

The knight disappeared again.

I can only see him when he moves! Tom realised. He searched the ground for his shield, but it was nowhere to be seen.

Elenna jumped to her feet. Tom saw his father stagger up, then drop to one knee. He ran and grabbed him by the arm. Tom steadied Taladon as his father climbed stiffly to his feet. He turned to Tom with a rueful smile.

"Ooof!"

Something crashed into Tom's back,

knocking the wind out of him and sending him sliding straight towards the fire raging in the entrance to Nanook's cave. Tom reached for his shield then remembered that he had dropped it. His hands and feet scrabbled uselessly on the ice. He couldn't stop his slide! The heat of the fire drove the breath from his throat. A red glow filled his vision and he heard Elenna scream.

Just as a roar of anger and despair swelled in Tom's throat, a powerful hand grabbed his cloak and spun him sideways away from the fire. The red glare and heat faded. Tom slid to a stop on the ice. He felt himself yanked to his feet.

"Son! Are you all right?" His father peered down at him and Tom realised what had happened. Taladon had used the speed of the golden boots to leap forwards and save him from a fiery death.

"Thank you," Tom gasped.

Taladon shook his head. "There was a time when the trickery of an invisible knight wouldn't have challenged me."

A harsh voice hissed across the icy plain. *"Then I'll fight you fairly!"*

Tom whirled around, lifting his sword. He narrowed his eyes, searching for the knight. "Where are you?" he muttered.

Elenna ran to join them, an arrow ready in her bow.

"I can't see him!" she cried.

"Look!" Tom pointed. There was no sign of the knight, but a large, sinister shape approached across the ice. The Varkule was bloody and battered.

It limped and its eyes blazed with hatred. They focused on Tom and the hideous creature gave a hacking laugh of pure evil.

Storm galloped to stand in front of Tom, snorting, but Tom could tell his horse was afraid of the Varkule. Where was the White Knight?

As if in answer, a figure in armour flickered into sight beside the Varkule. The creature had stopped advancing. It stood silently, flanks heaving as it glared at Tom and his companions. The shimmering outlines of the knight darkened and grew solid, until Tom could see him clearly. The White Knight jumped onto the Varkule's back, sitting astride it as though riding a horse.

Tom watched as a lance extended,

as though by magic, from the knight's
armour. It could only mean one
thing. Tom turned to Taladon.

"He wants to *joust*!"

CHAPTER SEVEN

WHITE AND GOLD

Tom knew what he had to do. The Varkule pawed the ground with its clawed feet. Drool dripped from its fangs. The White Knight sat upon its back, motionless, waiting.

"Find a way to put the fire out," Tom said to Elenna, his eyes never leaving the knight. "You and my father must free Nanook."

"While you do what?" Elenna asked.

"Put an end to this Beast Quest."
Tom said. He grabbed a long branch of
Frishwood that had rolled out of the
fire. It was almost perfectly straight,
and would do for a lance. But as he
turned to face the waiting knight, his
father caught hold of Tom's hand.

"Give it to me." Taladon's eyes
met Tom's and held them. "I wear
the Golden Armour. It is my task to
face the White Knight. I'll keep him
occupied – you free Nanook."

Tom opened his mouth to argue
but something stern and sad in his
father's eyes dried the words on his
tongue. Tom nodded. It would be
fine – no knight would ever defeat
Taladon. His father's strength and
courage would withstand any test.
"You'll need to borrow Storm," Tom
said. He whistled for the horse, which

trotted up to them.

Taladon held the Frishwood lance
lightly in one hand, testing its
balance. His golden armour shone in
the sunlight as he swung himself into
the saddle.

A bellow of rage rumbled from deep
inside the ice cave.

"Nanook!" Elenna cried.

Tom nodded, his stomach clenching

with worry for the Good Beast. Another chunk of the ice cave roof cracked and tumbled into the fire. Steam boiled up in hissing clouds as the flames ate away at the icy floor supporting the cave. They needed to put out the blaze soon, or Nanook's ice cave would collapse into the water beneath and the great Beast would perish.

A silver chime rang out. Following the sound, Tom spotted his shield, lying half-buried in snow a few paces away. He darted to collect it. As he picked it up, Nanook's bell rang again.

We're coming for you! Tom promised.

"We need water!" cried Elenna, shielding her eyes from the heat and glare.

"Or ice!" Tom replied. The fire had melted away the lower half of the cave entrance. An overhang of ice dripped onto the flames. "If we can bring down enough ice, it should put out the fire. Then Nanook can dig her way out!"

Tom pulled his sword from its scabbard. As he lifted it to carve into the ice, he glanced over at the knights. Taladon sat in Storm's saddle. The Varkule and Storm were galloping headlong towards each other. The stallion swept forward, Taladon's golden armour gleaming as he held his lance perfectly steady, pointing it at his enemy's heart. The Varkule bunched its high shoulders with each forward leap. The White Knight's lance jerked up and down with every step, yet he seemed glued to the creature's back as if by magic.

Tom held his breath. Taladon's

makeshift lance aimed true, but at the last moment, The White Knight kicked the Varkule's left flank, causing it to swerve. His lance knocked Taladon's Frishwood spear aside and slammed into the Beast Master's shoulder with a crash that echoed over the ice.

Tom gasped as the galloping animals raced past each other. Taladon

drooped in his saddle, his lance tip dragging across the ice.

"He's hurt!" Tom shouted, and started to run towards the jousting field.

"No, Tom!" Elenna shouted. "We must save Nanook!"

Tom paused, heart thudding. He felt torn in two. *Nanook needs me... But so does my father!* he thought.

Taladon straightened in his saddle. He gathered the reins and whirled Storm around. The stallion reared slightly on its hind legs, neighing a battle cry, then thundered back towards the Varkule and its deadly rider.

Tom spared his father one last glance, then turned back to his task. Elenna was right. There was nothing they could do right now. They had to save Nanook.

He edged into the fierce heat of the fire, lifted his sword and hacked at the ice overhang. Elenna took up a position on the other side of the fire, stabbing and slicing at the ice with the end of her bow. It was hard work. Tom's skin felt like it was crisping in the heat. Sweat poured into his eyes, and he had to blink it away before he could attack the ice once more.

Again he heard the double thunder of hooves and paws as the two jousters raced towards each other. He gouged at the wall in angry desperation. Gasping, Tom dared a glance over his shoulder. Pain sharp as a razor's edge sliced through him as he saw the White Knight's lance punch into his father's chest with such force that Taladon reeled in his saddle and nearly fell.

Tears blinded Tom. "No!" he cried.
He attacked the ice with all his rage.
*I will save Nanook and then help my
father defeat the evil knight. I must!*
Tom tugged his sword free of the ice
and lifted it again. This time in both
hands, preparing to drive it deep.
But before he could strike, the ice
groaned.

"Elenna, watch out!" Tom scrabbled
backwards. Blue splinters raced
up the wall of ice. Then, with a
crunching noise, the huge overhang
of ice crumpled and slid onto the fire.
Tom jumped out of the way just in
time, as the dying fire belched out
a gust of steam. They'd done it!

Elenna had jumped out of the
way just in time. She climbed to her
feet. The spot where she had stood
a moment before lay beneath an

avalanche of melting ice. "The fire is out," she said. "Nanook will be safe now. I'll help her dig herself out. You go and..." Her voice faded as she stared towards the battleground.

Tom whirled around. His breath caught in his throat as he saw Taladon leaning sideways out of the saddle, holding onto Storm's mane.

"Enough!" the White Night's grating voice rasped over the plain. *"You are obviously a mere mortal. Your flesh is weak. Find me a real challenger!"*

Instead of replying, Taladon leant further forwards and coughed. A patch of red bloomed upon the white ice and Tom's heart froze.

"You haven't won yet!" said Taladon thickly. He managed to pull himself straight in the saddle. "This battle will not be over until one of us has perished!" He lifted his lance and kicked his heels into Storm's sides. The stallion charged towards the White Knight.

Tom sprinted towards them, the sick feeling in his stomach growing heavier with every step. *Let it not be too late!* But even as the words rang inside his head, he knew in his heart that the battle between Taladon and the White Knight was nearly over.

CHAPTER EIGHT

A FATEFUL INHERITANCE

Crunch! The White Knight's lance speared Taladon high on the chest. Lifting him right out of the saddle and sending him crashing to the ground. He lay still, a golden sprawl on the snow.

Tom raced towards the spot where his father had fallen, his heart pounding in his ears. The only sounds were those of his running feet and the thud of the Varkule's paws on the ice.

Before Tom could reach his father, the White Knight wheeled the Varkule around, his lance held high in victory. He levelled the point and, kicking the Varkule viciously, galloped towards Taladon's unmoving body.

No! Tom realised what was happening. *The Knight is going to kill my father!* He ran but he was too late.

Taladon stirred, struggling to sit up.

"Stay down!" Tom heard himself shout. "Don't get up!"

If Taladon surrendered, the knight might show mercy. "Father! Stay down!" Tom cried again.

But Taladon pushed himself to his knees. The knight lowered his lance and sent it crashing into Taladon's chest. He flew backwards, sliding and tumbling across the ice in a tangle of limbs.

Tom had no breath left. He charged to where his father's body lay face down on the ice. Tom dropped onto his knees. His own shuddering gasps filled his ears. He grabbed his father's shoulders and turned him over. Inside his helmet, Taladon's face was deathly pale, his eyes shut.

Tom cradled his father's head in his arms. Taladon's eyes opened.

"Why?" Tom shouted, fighting to hold back the pain tearing at him. "Why did you keep fighting?" He fumbled at his belt, blinking tears from his eyes. *Where was it?* His fingers found Skor's jewel and he tugged it free. It had the power to heal broken bones. Tom clenched it hard in his fist and held it over Taladon, concentrating with all his might. *My father mustn't die! He must not!* thought Tom.

"No, Tom." The effort of speaking made Taladon wince with pain. He coughed, and blood dribbled from the corner of his mouth. "It's too late, son."

Tom stared into his father's eyes. It felt like the knight's lance had pierced his own heart. Taladon looked at him. The love in his eyes hurt Tom so much that he barely noticed the crash

of tons of ice collapsing or the ground
shaking. He only half-heard Nanook's
roar of triumph. Out of the corner
of his eye, he saw Elenna run past.
Beside her lumbered the huge, white
shape of Nanook. Tom grabbed his
father's hand and squeezed it.

He could barely hear Taladon's voice
over Nanook's roars and the Varkule's
squeals of terror.

"I did it for you, son," said his father, smiling. "The White Knight will imagine that after me, you will be easy." Taladon's smile was shattered by a cough. Fresh blood trickled down his chin. "You have the element of surprise," Taladon said. A spasm crossed his face. He took a slow, rasping breath. "Defeat the knight and you will finish the Quest, my son."

"I don't care about the Quest!" Tom almost shouted it. Fear was welling up and he struggled to contain it. "I'll get you help. Aduro must have a spell that—"

Taladon reached up a gauntlet-clad hand. He held it to Tom's cheek. "*Nothing* is more important than a Beast Quest. Always remember that. The Quest must continue…"

Tom blinked his tears away. They were

clouding his vision, making his father's face seem to fade from sight. The heavy weight of his father's head grew lighter. Tom tried to gather Taladon more tightly in his arms, but his father's body seemed to dissolve. Taladon's face blurred and was gone. Tom knelt, alone, on the ice, his arms empty.

Numb with shock, Tom stared at the place in the snow where his father had been only a breath ago. Thoughts tumbled through his mind. *What did it mean? Where was Taladon? Has he been magicked back to the palace? Is Aduro even now using his magic to save him?*

Tom raised his head, relief flooding through him. *Of course, that was the answer. Aduro was looking after Taladon!* Tom would make his father proud of him. He would finish this Quest, then join Taladon and stay with him until he was well again. Tom stood up…

…and a weight fell upon him. It pressed on his body, an unfamiliar heaviness. *What?* Tom looked down at himself. His warm cloak, his breeches and boots had disappeared. Instead, he was wearing a suit of Golden Armour.

The Golden Armour.

Tom gasped for breath, his heart drumming in his chest, and looked down at the armour, trying to understand. He felt the power of the Golden Armour take hold. A moment ago it had felt heavy, now it seemed feather-light. *It is the same. The Armour I fought for and won on my second Beast Quest. The Armour that I returned to Taladon when Father came back into his life. And that means…* Tom's thoughts focused on one fact. The truth cut into his heart.

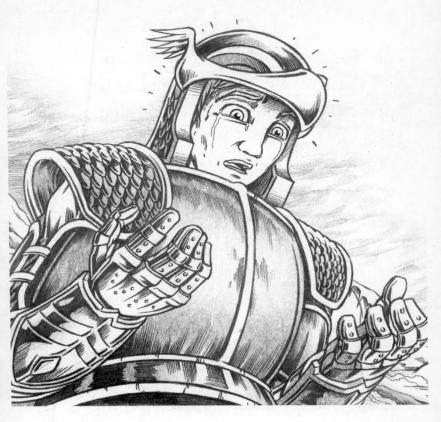

"*No!*"

Tom's cry rolled away to die in the
frozen vastness of the ice plain. Tom's
heart grew colder than the ice. The
Golden Armour was only worn by
the rightful Master of the Beasts.

That meant his father was dead.

CHAPTER NINE

VENGEANCE

"Tom!"

Elenna's voice cut through the mist in Tom's head. He dashed the tears from his eyes and turned to help his friend. He heard Nanook roaring. The great Beast was charging the White Knight, who still rode the Varkule. Nanook reached out a hairy arm to sweep the knight from the saddle.

The knight slapped the Varkule's flank

with the hilt of his lance, turning the monster so that it swept past Nanook and galloped straight at Elenna.

"Elenna, look out!" Tom cried, sprinting towards her.

She jumped back and shot an arrow at the Varkule as it lumbered past. The arrow dug into the creature's flanks. The Varkule roared and twisted, sliding to a halt and turning its head to bite at the arrow buried deep in its side. The White Knight flew from its back and crashed onto the ice. Tom raced towards his enemy, pulling his sword from its scabbard, but the White Knight's armour shimmered and he disappeared.

Nanook lumbered forward. She scowled, showing white fangs, and slammed a fearsome punch into the Varkule's face. The force of the blow

tossed the monster head over heels. It crashed onto the icy ground and lay still.

Suddenly there was a blur of movement and first Nanook and then Elenna were knocked flying. Tom spotted the White Knight's lance weaving across the ice. The knight himself remained almost invisible but the lance was easy to see because its tip was stained red with Taladon's blood!

Storm galloped up to Tom with Silver at his side. Tom knew his horse wanted to challenge the knight again. Tom's grief seemed to have frozen his heart. He reached up and stroked Storm's mane and his golden gauntlet glittered in the sunshine.

"We won't joust again, old friend," he said. "I will face the knight alone this time. Look after Elenna."

Tom tore across the ice. He used every ounce of power in the Armour and ran so fast he was a blur of gold. He harnessed the special vision of the golden helmet and the White Knight appeared in front of his eyes.

But as he closed in, the knight's armour began to swell. Tom heard the squeal of tortured metal as the white warrior's body doubled, tripled, and then tripled again until he towered above Tom. The knight grew round and broad. He dropped forward onto two powerful front legs and, with a final metallic screech, the White Knight became Tecton! The enormous creature had a thick leathery shell covered in enormous spikes. The spikes looked sharp enough to gouge holes in stone.

Tom felt no fear, only a cold determination. Tecton would pay! "While there's blood in my veins!" Tom's voice rang across the icy wasteland. "Nothing will stop me from avenging my father."

The Beast roared in answer. It rolled up and began to rumble across the snow like a spike-covered boulder, gathering speed, crunching everything in its path. Tom dodged out of the way. His fist, in the golden gauntlet, punched deep into Tecton's side. The Beast screamed in pain and fury. It uncurled its shell and slapped its tail against the ground, sending great cracks across the ice. Dozens of deadly spikes flew from its tail, hurtling through the air towards Tom.

Using the golden leg armour, Tom leapt high into the air. Tecton's spikes passed harmlessly beneath. Tom waited for the Beast to charge, then leapt out of the way as Tecton hurtled past. Each time, Tom crunched his fist into the Beast's armoured body. Every blow left a dent in Tecton's armour. The Beast roared with pain and retreated out of Tom's reach.

Tom spotted Elenna darting forward, an arrow nocked in her bow. Nanook

lumbered beside her, snarling in anger.
"No!" Tom shouted to them. "Keep
clear. This is my fight!"

Nanook shook her head in
disappointment, but stopped advancing.

"Why are you wearing the Golden
Armour?" Elenna shouted. She
backed away, but kept her arrow
trained on Tecton, who had circled to

face Tom again and was stamping the ground and roaring.

Tom had no time to reply. Grunting and snorting with fury, the Beast rolled itself into a ball of spikes. It rolled towards Tom. He leapt away, but Tecton swerved too. The Beast slammed into Tom, knocking him down. Tom staggered to his feet, but Tecton was already upon him. The Beast flattened him, crushing him into the ice. Tecton's weight pressed Tom into the ground, dozens of spikes punching into the Golden Armour, squeezing the breath from his body.

The pain was incredible, but Tom had no breath to scream. He felt the ice beneath his back begin to crack. Tecton rolled on and Tom lay motionless, gasping for air. He gathered his strength and crawled to his feet. Tecton was already wheeling around, starting to roll towards him. *Even the armour might not save me this time*, Tom realised.

"Tom!" A voice shrieked his name. He turned to see Elenna running towards him, waving an icicle-shaped diamond jewel. *Of course! One of the tokens!*

He heard Tecton rumbling closer. The ground shook beneath Tom's feet. The Beast was nearly upon him! Tom raced towards Elenna, using the power of his golden leg armour. As he neared her, Elenna threw the jewel. The diamond spun through the air towards him, a whirling rainbow of colour. Tom caught the jewel and clutched it tight. His heart swelling with determination, he turned to face his enemy.

"Come on then, Tecton! I'm ready for you!"

CHAPTER TEN

THE RIGHT PATH

Tecton's slashing spikes tore through the ice. Tom waited until the Beast was nearly on top of him, then dodged to one side and began to run. He harnessed the power of the golden leg armour and skimmed over the ground so fast his legs became a blur.

"Come on, you giant hedgehog! Try catching me!"

Tecton roared with fury and rolled

faster. But Tom ran faster. Then he
slowed slightly to allow the Beast
to nearly catch up. Tecton growled
and trundled towards him, but Tom
darted out of the way at the last
moment.

"Is that the best you can do?"
Tom shouted.

Tecton answered by unrolling and
stamping all four feet in turn. He
shook his head and roared in rage.
Then he curled into a ball again,
spinning across the ice. Tom raced
away, but now the Beast was moving
at a furious speed. Even though he
was using the power of the golden leg
armour, Tom was losing ground. The
rumbling behind him grew louder.
He felt the ground shake through
the soles of his armoured boots.
The sound of spikes slicing through

ice hurt his ears. He barely heard Elenna's cry of alarm.

Tom skidded to a stop and turned, carving a spray of ice with his heel. He held out the diamond. The Beast had no time to slow. It roared with terror and fear as Tom lunged to one side and dug the diamond into Tecton's armour as the Beast hurtled past. The diamond sliced through the armoured shell with a grating metallic scream. The force nearly tore the diamond from Tom's hand.

He had wounded the Beast! Tecton slowly wheeled round to face Tom once more, leaving a trail of red on the ice. Grunting and growling, the Beast gathered speed, whirling across the ice with slashing spikes. Tom dodged to one side, but Tecton had guessed his game! The Beast swerved too, rolling straight at him. Tom slashed out with the diamond, digging it hard into the armoured flesh.

The Beast bellowed in pain. It veered to one side of Tom, nearly knocking him down, snapping several spikes on Tom's Golden Armour. As Tecton shot past, its thick shell slid off its body and broke apart.

Tom dropped the diamond. Blood was pounding in his head. He saw his enemy – the creature that had killed his father – lying helpless before him on the ground. Tom strode over the ice, hearing it crunch beneath his feet. The blood sang louder in Tom's head. He drew his sword. "Now," he told the creature lying before him, "I will avenge my father!"

Tecton's body was shrinking and dissolving. As Tom reached him,

Tecton disappeared completely. In his place lay the White Knight.

Once so invincible, the Knight of Forton lay face down on the ice. He was gasping and spitting blood just as Taladon had done only moments before. The memory of his father, dying in his arms, clouded Tom's eyes. He shook his head to clear it, gripping the hilt of his sword more tightly. He stared down at his foe, and his heart held no pity. He'd never wanted revenge on any of the Beasts, until now. *This is what Tecton has done to me,* he thought grimly.

Tom raised his sword.

Somewhere behind him, he heard Elenna shout: "No!"

Tom did not hesitate. He drove his sword towards the White Knight. But there was no crunch of steel

slicing through armour, flesh and
bone. Tom's blade struck only ice.
The White Knight has disappeared!
Furious, Tom spun round. Who had
stolen his foe from him?

"Tom!"

Aduro flickered into sight, an apparition floating just above the ice. The wizard looked at Tom, both understanding and disappointment in his eyes. Tom glared back.

"You've taken the knight!" Tom growled.

"He is back in the Gallery of Tombs," replied Aduro. "It's where he belongs."

"You have no right," Tom shouted. "He killed my father!"

Tom jumped as a hand touched his wrist. He nearly struck out, but saw in time that it was Elenna.

"Give me your sword," she said. Tom stared at her, and then loosened his grip. He let her take the sword.

"This is not the way, Tom," said Aduro. The wizard's voice was quiet, but stern. "Vengeance is *never* the way. You know that."

Tom shook his head. "The White Knight will pay for what he's done!" But even as he said these words, guilt curled around his heart.

"No, Tom," Aduro replied. "The White Knight is not responsible for Taladon's death." The wizard gave him a searching look. "You know that, if you are honest with yourself. Do not let anger and grief cloud your vision."

Tom felt his hatred and fury loosen its hold. He nodded. Aduro was right. It was Malvel who must be punished. All this was the Evil Wizard's doing.

Tom looked at Aduro. "I have one more knight and one more Beast to defeat," he said. "Then I will make sure that Malvel will never again visit his evil on this kingdom, or any other!"

Tom turned to look across the
snow-swept plains. "Malvel will
pay for what he has done."

Aduro nodded and sighed. "You
must come back to the Palace now,
you and Elenna. We have much to
discuss." The wizard faded from sight
as quickly as a candle blown out by
the wind.

Tom gazed around him. The blue

of the northern sky was fading to grey. Snow floated gently down. Nanook approached him, her white bulk towering over him. Her dark eyes were sorrowful. For the first time since his father's death, Tom felt warmth kindle in his heart. He smiled at the good Beast. "Thank you for your help, Nanook. Sleep well, my friend!"

The Beast nodded and turned away. As she lumbered across the snow towards the remains of her ice cave, Nanook gave a wide berth to the body of the Varkule, which was already disappearing beneath a dusting of snow. Elenna gathered her arrows and called to Storm and Silver.

Tears pricked Tom's eyes as he looked down at the golden plates that covered his body. He had dreamed of one day wearing this Golden Armour and following in his father's footsteps. He had looked forward to becoming the Master of the Beasts, but that day had come too soon.

"The rest of the Quest is for you, Father," he said into the icy air. "I'll save Avantia for you."

Join Tom on the next stage
of the Beast Quest when he meets

DOOMSKULL
THE KING OF FEAR

Win an exclusive
Beast Quest T-shirt and goody bag!

Tom has battled many fearsome Beasts and we want to know which one is your favourite! Send us a drawing or painting of your favourite Beast and tell us in 30 words why you think it's the best.

Each month we will select **three** winners to receive a Beast Quest T-shirt and goody bag!

Send your entry on a postcard to
BEAST QUEST COMPETITION
Orchard Books, 338 Euston Road, London NW1 3BH.

Australian readers should email:
childrens.books@hachette.com.au

New Zealand readers should write to:
Beast Quest Competition, PO Box 3255, Shortland St,
Auckland 1140, NZ or email: childrensbooks@hachette.co.nz

**Don't forget to include your name and address.
Only one entry per child.**

Good luck!

Join the Quest,
Join the Tribe

www.beastquest.co.uk

Have you checked out the Beast Quest website?
It's the place to go for games, downloads, activities,
sneak previews and lots of fun!

You can read all about your favourite Beasts, down-
load free screensavers and desktop wallpapers for
your computer, and even challenge your friends
to a Beast Tournament.

Sign up to the newsletter at www.beastquest.co.uk
to receive exclusive extra content and the oppor-
tunity to enter special members-only competitions.
We'll send you up-to-date info on all the Beast
Quest books, including the next exciting series
which features six brand-new Beasts!

Get 30% off all Beast Quest Books at www.beastquest.co.uk
Enter the code BEAST at the checkout.

All books priced at £4.99,
special bumper editions
priced at £5.99.

Orchard Books are available from all good bookshops, or can
be ordered from our website: www.orchardbooks.co.uk,
or telephone 01235 827702, or fax 01235 8227703.

FREE COLLECTOR CARDS INSIDE!

Series 10: MASTER OF THE BEASTS
COLLECT THEM ALL!

An old enemy has come back to haunt Tom –
and unleash six awesome new Beasts!

NOCTILA
THE DEATH OWL

978 1 40831 518 7

SHAMANI
THE RAGING FLAME

978 1 40831 519 4

LUSTOR
THE ACID DART

978 1 40831 520 0

VOLTREX
THE TWO-HEADED OCTOPUS

978 1 40831 521 7

TECTON
THE ARMOURED GIANT

978 1 40831 522 4

DOOMSKULL
THE KING OF FEAR

978 1 40831 523 1

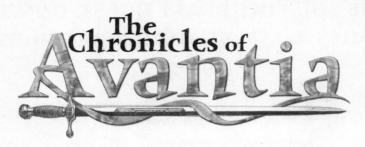

The Chronicles of Avantia

FROM THE DARK, A HERO ARISES...

Dare to enter the kingdom of Avantia.

A new evil arises in Avantia. Lord Derthsin has ordered his armies into the four corners of Avantia. If the four Beasts of Avantia can find their Chosen Riders they might have the strength to challenge Derthsin. But if they fail, the land of Avantia will be lost forever...

FIRST HERO, CHASING EVIL, CALL TO WAR, FIRE AND FURY-
OUT NOW!

www.chroniclesofavantia.com